Mythical Creatures
DRAGONS

by Theresa Jarosz Alberti

FOCUS READERS

FOCUS READERS

www.focusreaders.com

Focus Readers is distributed by North Star Editions:
sales@northstareditions.com | 888-417-0195

Produced for Focus Readers by Red Line Editorial.

Photographs ©: adike/Shutterstock Images, cover, 1; Sylphe_7/iStockphoto, 4–5; Fotokostic/Shutterstock Images, 7; e71lena/iStockphoto, 8–9; ChameleonsEye/ Shutterstock Images, 11, 29; Harbar Liudmyla/Shutterstock Images, 13; FairytaleDesign/ iStockphoto, 14–15; Kostyantyn Ivanyshen/Shutterstock Images, 16; Sofiaworld/ Shutterstock Images, 19; Kit Korzun/Shutterstock Images, 20–21; Melkor3D/Shutterstock Images, 22–23, 25; Refluo/Shutterstock Images, 26

ISBN
978-1-63517-900-2 (hardcover)
978-1-64185-002-5 (paperback)
978-1-64185-204-3 (ebook pdf)
978-1-64185-103-9 (hosted ebook)

Library of Congress Control Number: 2018931701

Printed in the United States of America
Mankato, MN
May, 2018

About the Author

Theresa Jarosz Alberti called herself a writer when she was 10 years old. She wrote many stories and poems. Now she enjoys writing for both kids and adults. She lives in Minneapolis, Minnesota.

TABLE OF CONTENTS

CHAPTER 1

BEWARE THE DRAGON

High in the mountains, all is quiet. A dragon naps on a nest of sticks and weeds. Three golden eggs lie beneath her enormous green body. The dragon keeps the eggs warm.

Dragons' wings allow them to live on even the tallest mountains.

She dreams of dragon **hatchlings** soon to come.

A rustle of leaves wakes the dragon. Her head snaps up. She sees a flash of silver. A knight has come to fight her. He wants to protect his village from the fiery beast. Many brave knights have come before and failed.

The knight raises his sword high. The dragon opens her mouth and breathes a blast of fire. The battle begins.

 In fantasy stories, dragons and knights are often enemies.

CHAPTER 2

DRAGONS FOR EVERYONE

Dragons are mighty **mythical** creatures. People have told stories about dragons for thousands of years. Most countries have their own unique dragon stories.

Many dragon stories take place near castles.

In Western countries, dragons are fierce fire-breathers. The West includes countries in Europe, North America, and South America. In Eastern countries, dragons are wise and powerful **serpents**. The East includes countries in Asia.

FUN FACT

In China, people make dragon puppets from wood and cloth. These long, colorful dragons dance in parades on the Chinese New Year.

 Chinese dancers use long poles to handle dragon puppets. They perform a dragon dance.

Scientists found one of the oldest dragon images in a Chinese **tomb**. The image may be 6,000 years old.

The piece of art was made from colored seashells.

Other dragon images appear on old maps. Hundreds of years ago, people thought the world was flat. They believed dragons lived at the edge of the world. Fear of dragons kept them from exploring the world.

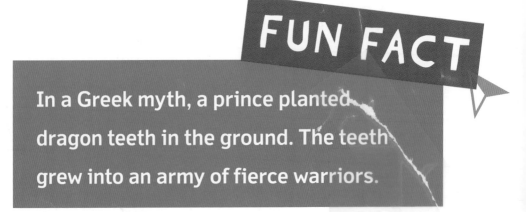

FUN FACT

In a Greek myth, a prince planted dragon teeth in the ground. The teeth grew into an army of fierce warriors.

 This map shows dragons at the edge of the world.

No one knows how dragon stories came to be. Some scientists think ancient people found dinosaur bones. Back then, people did not know about dinosaurs. They may have thought the bones belonged to dragons.

CHAPTER 3

LIZARD LOOKS

Dragons in Western countries are frightening creatures. They have huge, lizard-like bodies. These dragons have long necks, sharp claws, and strong tails. **Scales** cover the beasts from head to tail.

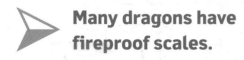

Many dragons have fireproof scales.

 Dragons have long, lizard-like tongues.

The dragons' scales are often a mix of colors. They can be red, blue, green, silver, or gold.

Western dragons have two wings. Most Western dragons have four legs. But others have only two legs.

Some dragons with two legs are called wyverns. Wyverns also have spiked tails.

Dragons in Eastern countries have long bodies and very short legs. Most Eastern dragons don't have wings. However, some of them can fly.

FUN FACT

The hydra is a type of dragon in Greek mythology. This mighty dragon has nine or more heads.

People compare Eastern dragons to many animals. The dragon's head looks like the head of a camel. And its body looks like a snake. The dragon also has claws like an eagle and scales like a fish.

Eastern dragons can be almost any color. Images often show the

FUN FACT

Southeast Asian **folklore** tells of dragon-like creatures called nagas. Nagas have snake-like bodies and human heads.

 In China, red dragons stand for happiness, passion, and creativity.

dragon with a wide-open mouth.

This makes it seem as if the dragon

is laughing.

DRAGONS TODAY

The Komodo dragon is a **monitor lizard** named after dragons. It lives on Komodo Island in Indonesia. Komodo dragons can grow as long as 10 feet (3.0 m). Some weigh as much as 300 pounds (136 kg). A Komodo dragon has scaly skin, a snout, and a strong tail. It hunts large animals for food.

Sea dragons are also named after dragons. These small fish live in oceans near Australia. Leafy sea dragons are covered in leaf-shaped flaps. Weedy sea dragons have fewer flaps. Both look like small, colorful dragons.

The Komodo dragon uses its long tongue to catch prey.

CHAPTER 4

DRAGON POWERS

Many dragons make their **lairs** in caves, mountains, or forests. But some ▓▓▓▓▓ live by rivers or lakes. Dragons usually live with other dragons. Communities of dragons are known as weyrs.

 Dragons may attack castles, villages, and homes.

Weyrs grow when female dragons lay eggs. Female dragons sit on their nests to protect the eggs.

Western dragons are wicked and dangerous. They breathe fire and have **poisonous** breath. Hungry dragons might eat sheep, cows, or humans. T█████████ piles of treasure, such as gold or jewels. Some stories mention castles, knights, and princesses. Dragons in these stories fight humans to protect themselves.

 Dragons hide their treasure in caves and dungeons.

Eastern dragons are water spirits. These dragons rule over oceans and lakes. They breathe clouds and mist. They also control the weather.

Many Eastern dragons chase after a red ball, or pearl. The pearl gives them wisdom.

In many stories, Eastern dragons help and protect humans. They bring humans good luck.

Chinese dragons have many magical powers. They can make themselves as small as a worm. Or they can grow as large as the world. Some Chinese dragons turn into water or fire. Others can become invisible or glow in the dark.

FUN FACT

Dragons are popular in movies and books. For example, dragons appear in *The Hobbit*, the Harry Potter series, and *Shrek*.

FOCUS ON
DRAGONS

Write your answers on a separate piece of paper.

1. Write a sentence that describes one difference between Eastern and Western dragons.

2. Why do you think dragon stories are so popular?

3. Where was one of the earliest dragon images found?
   - **A.** on a map
   - **B.** in a tomb
   - **C.** in a cave

4. How are mythical dragons and Komodo dragons similar?
   - **A.** They both live in North America.
   - **B.** They both have scales.
   - **C.** They both have magical powers.

5. What does **ancient** mean in this book?

*Some scientists think **ancient** people found dinosaur bones. Back then, people did not know about dinosaurs.*

    A. from a long time ago
    B. from a short time ago
    C. from the future

6. What does **communities** mean in this book?

Dragons usually live with other dragons.
***Communities** of dragons are known as weyrs.*

    A. babies or eggs
    B. armies going into battle
    C. groups that live together

Answer key on page 32.

GLOSSARY

folklore
Fictional stories that people pass down over the years.

hatchlings
Young animals that are born from eggs.

lairs
Homes or resting places of animals.

monitor lizard
A large reptile found mainly in Africa, Asia, and Australia.

mythical
Having to do with fictional stories or myths.

poisonous
Deadly or harmful.

scales
The thin, flat, overlapping pieces of hard skin that cover the bodies of fish and reptiles.

serpents
Large, snake-like creatures.

tomb
A large stone structure that holds a dead body.

TO LEARN MORE

BOOKS

Loh-Hagan, Virginia. *Dragons: Magic, Myth, and Mystery*. Ann Arbor, MI: Cherry Lake Publishing, 2017.

Sautter, A. J. *Discover Dragons, Giants, and Other Deadly Fantasy Monsters*. Mankato, MN: Capstone Press, 2018.

Sherman, Jill. *Komodo Dragons*. North Mankato, MN: Capstone Press, 2017.

NOTE TO EDUCATORS

Visit **www.focusreaders.com** to find lesson plans, activities, links, and other resources related to this title.

INDEX

Answer Key: 1. Answers will vary; 2. Answers will vary; 3. B; 4. B; 5. A; 6. C